A **SporTellers**™ Book

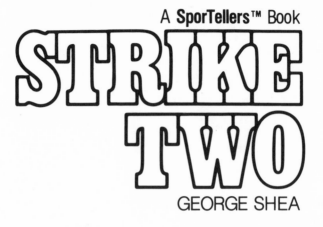

STRIKE TWO

GEORGE SHEA

 CHILDRENS PRESS, CHICAGO

SporTellers™

Catch the Sun
Fear on Ice
Foul Play
High Escape
Play-Off
Race to Win
Strike Two
Stroke of Luck

Childrens Press Edition
Senior development editor: Christopher Ransom Miller
Content editor: Carol B. Whiteley
Production editor: Mary McClellan
Design manager: Eleanor Mennick
Illustrator: Bob Haydock
Cover: Bob Haydock

ISBN 0-516-02267-9
Library of Congress Catalog Card Number: 80–82990
Printed in the United States of America.
1.9   8   7   6   5   4   3   2   1

Contents

1 Playing Slow and Easy 1
2 The Past and the Present 8
3 New Team 16
4 Pulling Them Out 21
5 Stealing Home 28
6 Going Strong 33
7 The Story Gets Out 39
8 One More Time 47
9 Clearing the Fence 54

Playing Slow and Easy *1*

Al Sanchez stood in the on-deck circle waiting for his turn at bat. His team, the Hanson Rockets, was playing the AC Auto Tool Blues. It was a semipro game—a night game in an old ball park. As Al looked around, he saw that there weren't even a hundred people in the stands. It wasn't a very important game to baseball fans in St. Louis. But it was important to Al. In fact, it could be the most important game he would ever play—if the man from the Cards showed up.

Al watched as the batter before him hit an easy pop-up that was caught by the Blues' shortstop. Now it was Al's turn to hit. Before he stepped up to the plate, Frank Martino, the

Rockets' manager, called him back. Al stood on the dugout steps as Martino took his arm.

"The man from the Cards is here," Martino said. "I just saw him come in."

Al turned his head to look at the half-empty stands. "Where?"

"Never mind," said Martino. "That's not important. What is important is that he's from the Cards—the big time—and he has come to see *you* play. Now get up there and knock the ball out of the park."

When Martino finished speaking, Al turned and started toward the plate. But in a second, Martino called out again. "One more thing," he said. "Stay out of trouble tonight. Show this guy you know how to handle yourself."

Al stepped into the batter's box. His mouth was dry. He wanted to show the man from the Cards how good he was.

The first pitch was a fastball, low and outside. Al let it go by. "Strike," the umpire called. Al didn't like the call, but he didn't say anything.

The next pitch was a slow curve. Al didn't like the look of it, either. He let it go past. "Strike," the umpire called again.

Now Al was really nervous. He shook his head and tapped his bat against the plate a few times. I can't strike out, he thought. Not tonight. I've got to hit the next one.

The next pitch was a fastball, high and outside. But it was close enough for Al. He swung and smashed the ball over the shortstop's head. He had a clean single. But when the left fielder was slow coming up with the ball, Al decided to keep going.

He went into second at top speed and slid under the throw. Dirt flew up all around him. But through the dirt, Al saw the umpire give the safe sign.

Getting to his feet, Al brushed himself off. Then he looked at Martino, who was standing in the dugout. The gray-haired manager lifted his hat and put it back on, the sign for the steal. Al took off with the next pitch, heading for third. Then he heard the crack of the bat, and the ball went past the first baseman into right field. The noise of the crowd filled Al's ears as he rounded third and dug for home.

Al could see the Blues' catcher standing in front of home plate. The catcher was waiting for the throw from right field. When it came, it was low and on the mark. It had Al beat. But Al wouldn't believe it. He threw himself at the catcher. The catcher went down, dropping the ball as he fell. Al fell over the catcher's legs, kept going on all fours, and touched home. He was safe, and the Rockets were ahead 1–0.

The next batter for the Rockets made the third out, and the team moved to the field. Al took up his place at third base, where he always played. But he wished he were back at bat. He knew he wasn't a very good fielder. He had never been very happy there.

The Blues' first batter hit a hard ground ball right to Al. Al knocked it down, picked it up, and threw in a hurry to first. The throw was high. The first baseman jumped to catch the ball, but it sailed way over his head. The runner didn't stop until he got to second.

Great, Al thought. He looked at the stands and kicked the dirt. I'm sure the guy from the Cards loved that, he thought. I should have held on to the ball. You can't make a good throw when you do it in a hurry.

The next batter came up to the plate. He hit a high fly to short right. One out. The batter after that popped up to the catcher. Two outs. Al knew the man on second would be running on anything.

The count went to three balls and two strikes, as the Blues' fourth batter tried to get on base. He kept getting a piece of the ball. Then he got more than a piece. He hit the ball high and hard to third. Al jumped into the air to catch it, but it was way over his head. The runner rounded third as Al turned to take the cutoff throw from the outfield. It came fast. Al grabbed it, wheeled around, and fired the ball to the plate. The Blues' runner tried a hard slide to beat the throw. But the umpire called him out.

Play went on, with the Rockets scoring 2 runs and the Blues answering with 3. Finally, Al was up again. He drove in another run with a long single to right. His next time at bat, the bases were full, and he hit a double off the wall in center. The play scored all three runners. When the inning ended, the Rockets were ahead 7–3, and Al felt good. He had knocked in or scored 5 of his team's 7 runs.

Then he made another bad play at third. He took his eyes off a throw, and the ball rocketed past him. Two runners scored. Now it was 7–5, and Al stormed back to the dugout at the end of the inning.

"Forget it," said Martino, as Al started calling himself all kinds of names. "Use your bat to get those runs back."

He came up with two outs and runners on second and third. The Blues' pitcher gave Al a long, hard look. Then he came in with the first pitch. It was a fastball, high and inside. It came right at Al's head. He dropped and hit the dirt. When he got up, he was mad. Picking up the bat, he took a few steps toward the pitcher. Then he remembered what Martino had said: *Stay out of trouble tonight.* He stopped, looked hard at the pitcher, and then stepped back into the batter's box. From the dugout he could hear Martino shouting "Come on, Al! Hit the ball! Don't him *him!*"

The next pitch was right where Al wanted it—over the plate and high enough to hit. Al swung hard and drove the ball past the fence in deep center field. He dropped the bat and followed his two teammates slowly around the bases, the calls from the crowd in his ears. When he reached home plate, Frank Martino was waiting with a smile and a welcome. "You've got it now, kid," he said. "You're on your way to the big time!"

"I'll believe it when I see it," said Al. But he was smiling just the same.

The Blues got a quick run in the ninth, but then the batters went down one, two, three. It was over. The Rockets had won 10–6.

As he walked off the field, Al felt good— good but nervous. What would happen next? Where was the man from the Cardinals? Would he want to talk to Al? And where was Martino? Al looked around for him, but he wasn't in sight.

Suddenly Al began to feel hurt and angry. Who am I kidding? I'm not going to make it into pro ball, he thought. They wouldn't give me a chance before. Why should they now? Standing next to the dugout, he watched the fans move slowly out of the park. "It will never happen," he said out loud as he headed for the locker room. Then he heard his name being called.

"Al, come here! Where are you going?" It was Frank Martino. "There's a man here who wants to talk to you!"

CHAPTER 2

The Past and the Present

Al turned and saw Martino standing near the fence at the bottom of the stands with a short man with brown hair. The two men watched Al as he walked over to them.

"Al, I want you to meet Norm Corwin," Martino said. "Norm is with the St. Louis Cardinals."

Al smiled as he shook Corwin's hand. "Pleased to meet you," he said. It was finally happening.

"Nice game you played tonight," Corwin told Al. "I'd like to talk to you about it—and some other things."

"Sure," said Al. "Let's go up into the stands."

"You guys go on ahead," Frank Martino told them. He looked at Al and tapped his arm. "See you later."

Al Sanchez and Norm Corwin climbed a few rows into the stands and sat down on a hard bench. Corwin pushed back his hat and turned to Al.

"The story is this, Al," said Corwin. "I like the way you played ball tonight. You play to win. You can hit *and* run. Your fielding isn't much, but you've got a good arm. With work you could turn into a pretty fair fielder. I'd say you're one of the best young players I've seen in a long time."

Corwin stopped talking and looked out over the field. Then he began to speak again.

"You're good all right," he said. "But—"

Al broke in. "But what?"

"But you've been in a lot of trouble," Corwin said. "I don't know if the Cards can take a chance on you."

Al felt his insides sinking into his shoes. It was happening all over again. He took a deep breath. When he let it out, he was very angry. He got to his feet and looked down at Corwin. "Is that why you came here tonight? Just to

tell me that you can't take a chance on me?"

Corwin looked up at him. "Take it easy, Al," he said. "I came here because Frank Martino asked me to come to see you play. Frank's an old friend. And he really believes in you."

Al sat back down. He was shaking. That's it, he thought. No one is ever going to give me a chance to play. No one.

Only a year before, things had been very different. Six teams in the big leagues had been after him to sign with them. The Giants had said they would give him $90,000 to play with their team. Everyone had wanted him.

Then he got into trouble. He had started hanging out with a new group of people. They were wild, but Al liked them. One night he borrowed a car from someone in the crowd. Later that night, the police stopped him on the road. They told him that the car he was driving had been stolen. Later they got a warrant to search the car. Inside it, they found drugs and a loaded gun.

Al was arrested. He couldn't believe it. He had not known that the car had been stolen. And he didn't know anything about the gun or the drugs. But the police didn't believe his story. And the man who had given Al the car had dropped out of sight.

Al went to jail for a year. When he got out, only Frank Martino and the Rockets would let him play ball with them. None of the teams in the big leagues would even talk to him.

Now he sat in the empty stands beside the man from the St. Louis Cardinals, and it looked like the same old story. "So, Frank made you come," Al said. "You're only here to make him happy. The Cards don't really want me."

"I didn't say that," said Corwin. "But I will say that I think you got a bad deal on that drug thing. You're a good player, Al. And I think it's about time you were playing for a good team. I'd like to see you with the Cardinals. But I'll have to talk to the front office first. Are you willing to start out at low pay?"

"Last year the Giants wanted to give me $90,000 to sign with them." Al was getting angry again.

"That was last year," said Corwin. "Now I think you'll have to take what you can get. And if I were you, I wouldn't turn down anything the Cards think is fair. This is probably the last chance you'll ever get to play pro ball."

"All right," said Al. "All right. See what you can do." He knocked the dirt from the bottom of his green and white shoes. Then he stood up. "I know this is my last chance. Thanks for helping. I'll wait for you to call me."

Al went home and waited. The inside of his small room felt like jail all over again. What would happen when Corwin spoke to the Cards? Al could think about nothing but that.

Then, a few days later, the telephone rang. It was Norm Corwin.

"I've got a deal for you, Al," he said. "The Cards want you to play for their farm team down in Woodside. The money you'll be playing for isn't much, but—"

Al cut in. "What about a bonus?"

"They'll give you a $10,000 bonus—*if* you get through the season all right. I have a feeling they'll up it to $15,000 if you do really well down there."

Al let out the deep breath he had been holding. "OK," he said. "That sounds OK to me." Suddenly he smiled. He felt good for the first time in a long time. He was back in baseball—on his way to the big leagues.

"Just be careful, Al," Corwin went on. "Even if you got a bad deal the first time, the Cards will get rid of you if there's any sign of trouble again. No matter who's right and who's wrong."

"I've got the picture," Al told Corwin. "But there's not going to be any more trouble." He thanked Corwin and hung up the telephone.

Sitting down in a chair, Al let out another deep breath. He looked slowly around the room. There wasn't much to see. He had always been poor. He had always lived in the worst parts of the city. Now there was a chance that things could be different. And all he had to do was make it through a season doing what he loved best—playing baseball.

The next day, Al Sanchez signed on with the Cardinals. The day after that, he got on a bus and headed for Woodside. He watched out the window as farmhouses and beautiful old trees moved past. He saw lazy dogs and children on the side of small-town streets.

It was afternoon when the big bus finally pulled into Woodside. When Al stepped off the bus, he found himself in a hot, dusty town with low, white buildings.

Inside the dark bus station it was cool. The map on the station wall pointed out the Woodside playing field, and Al started to head that way. In a few minutes he saw a fenced field with a big sign in front of it. *Hawks Field,* the sign read. *Home of the Woodside Hawks, St. Louis Cardinals' Rookie League Farm Team.*

Al walked inside the gate and found the Woodside team working out on the dry field. An older, heavyset man stood at home plate, batting out fly balls to the players. When he saw Al, he stopped and called out to him: "You—what do you want here?"

"I'm Al Sanchez," Al called back. "I just came down from St. Louis."

The man threw down the bat. "Take over," he ordered a player standing near him. Then he walked over to Al. "Follow me, Sanchez," he said. He headed across the field toward a small building. Al had to walk fast to keep up with him.

When they reached the building, the older man led Al down some steps and into a dark red room. It held a beat-up desk and a few chairs. The man sat down behind the desk and put his feet up on it.

"I'm Gus Waller," he said. "I'm the manager of this team. This—"

"Pleased to meet you," Al broke in.

"Well, Sanchez, I'm not sure that I'm pleased to meet you," Gus Waller went on. "I know all about you. And from what I've heard, I know that I don't need you or your kind on my team."

New Team *3*

Al fixed Waller with a hard look. "What do you know about me? I just signed a deal with the Cards," he said. "I'm supposed to *play* down here."

"You have signed a little piece of paper with the Cards, Sanchez," Gus Waller shouted back. "They decided that you're *good enough* to play on my team." Then Waller's voice got low. "But who do you think decides *if* you play? *I* do. And I'm not sure I want a guy who makes trouble and spends time in jail to play at all."

Al started toward Waller, but then he stopped. "I just have one question," Al said. "Are you going to give me a chance to play or not? Because if you're not—"

"You'll get your chance," Waller said. Then he stood up and looked hard into Al's eyes.

"But don't you make any trouble down here. You break one of my rules just once and you're gone. You understand me?"

"I understand you," said Al. "Now when do I start playing ball?"

Waller headed for the door. "We have a game tonight at 7:30," he said. "You play third base, right?"

"Right," said Al.

"Too bad," Waller said, turning to look back at Al. "I've already got a good third baseman. Guy named Willis. So for now you're just going to sit on the bench and wait your turn." Then Waller stopped and scratched the back of his head. "You ever catch? I could use another catcher right now."

"I'm not a catcher," Al said. "I came here to play third base."

"We'll see about it," Waller said. "Right now, all you've got to do is read this." He handed Al a small book with the team's rules in it. "I'll explain the signs to you before the game tonight. Now get out of here. You'll be staying in room 322 at the Prince Hotel." Waller fixed Al with a hard look. "You know any Japanese?"

"No," said Al.

"Great," Waller said. "You'll be rooming with a guy named Tanimoto. He doesn't speak any English. You should be able to get along just fine with him."

With the manager's words ringing in his ears, Al left the ball park and walked to the hotel. He lay down on the bed there and tried to get some sleep. But he couldn't. He was too keyed up. He didn't think he was going to like playing for Waller—if he got a chance to play at all. At six o'clock he grabbed something to eat and set out for the ball park.

For the first time in his life, Al wasn't on the starting lineup. And he didn't like it. He was hot and angry as the rest of his team got ready to play the Coaxwood Pirates, a Pittsburgh Pirates farm team.

The game began with the first Coaxwood batter hitting a hard smash to third. Scott Willis, the Hawks' third baseman, moved quickly to his left and came up with the ball. He fired it across to first to make the out.

"Willis comes up with some nice plays," the player sitting on the bench next to Al said.

"He looks OK out there," Al said.

"I'm Lou Clayton," the player told Al. "I guess you just got in today."

"That's right," said Al. "I'm Al Sanchez. I just came down from St. Louis."

Lou shook Al's hand. "I'm one of the pitchers," he said. "What position do you play, Al?"

"Third base," Al answered.

Lou shook his head. "That's too bad," he said. "You might be sitting on this bench for a long time. Waller likes Willis's game a lot. We have been playing two weeks, and he's started Willis at third every game.

Al nodded to Lou Clayton. Maybe that will change, he thought.

Play went on, and the Coaxwood team was leading. Soon Scott Willis came to the plate. The bases were loaded, and there was only one out. Willis could tie up the game if he brought in 2 runs.

Al felt torn as Willis got ready to hit. Part of Al wanted the Hawks to score some runs. Another part of him wanted to see Willis hit into a double play.

Al didn't have much time to worry about it. Willis struck out on three pitches. Then the next batter fouled out.

The Hawks were still behind by 2 runs as they came to bat in the bottom of the ninth. The first batter got on with a single, and the next one walked. With Neal Tanimoto, the pitcher, set to bat next, Waller needed a pinch hitter.

"Sanchez!"

Al almost jumped when Waller called his name. He got up and walked over to where Waller stood at the end of the dugout.

"How are you feeling, Sanchez?" The manager looked out at the field as he spoke. He didn't wait for an answer. "You wanted a chance to play. This is it. It should be easy for a big star like you. Let's see if you can do anything out there."

Al grabbed a bat and walked up to the plate. He took a deep breath and checked the field. The two Hawks runners were taking strong leads, dancing off first and second. The Coaxwood outfield was moving back.

Al took a long, hard look at the pitcher before he stepped into the batter's box. Then he took two slow practice swings with the bat. He watched as the pitcher got ready to throw.

Pulling Them Out 4

The pitch came in—high and inside—right at Al's head. He hit the dirt. When he got up, he dusted himself off and stepped out of the batter's box. Slowly he looked out at the pitcher.

The young Coaxwood pitcher was smiling at him. Al gave him a mean look and pounded the plate a few times with his bat. He waited out the next pitch—a curve, low and outside. The count went to two balls and no strikes.

Looking over to Waller for a sign, Al saw the manager run his fingers across the front of his shirt. It was the take sign. Waller probably thought that the pitcher was losing his control. He wanted Al not to swing at the next pitch. He wanted him to take the next pitch and to try to draw a walk.

Al dug in as he waited for the pitch. It was a fastball, a little high and right down the middle. It had home run written all over it. But Al held back. "Strike!" the umpire called.

Al looked over to Waller again. The manager had his arms folded across his chest. The take sign was off.

The next pitch came in—another fastball. Just where Al wanted it. He swung hard and smashed it out to deep right field. It sailed over the right fielder's head and went rolling toward the fence.

As the right fielder chased the ball, the Woodside runners took off from first and second. As Al rounded first, he could see the lead runner rounding third. One run would score for sure.

Al slowed a bit as he neared second, looking for the throw from right field. But no throw was coming yet. He picked up speed. As he closed on third, he saw the Coaxwood catcher running after a bad throw to home. A second run was scoring. Al tore for the plate.

He was almost there when the catcher came up with the ball. Both men were only 10 feet from the plate. The catcher looked up, surprised to see Al coming. He ran to block the plate. Al slid hard, pulling his left leg around the catcher's body. The tag was too late. Al was safe with the winning run. The Hawks had won the game 5–4.

A happy shout went up from the stands. Players rushed out of the dugout and crowded around Al. There was a lot of laughing and calling as everyone shook his hand and hit him on the back.

"Hey, we'll have to keep you around, Sanchez!" Lou Clayton shouted at him.

It was all over in a minute. Waller didn't come over to shake his hand. But for the first time, Al caught a small smile on the manager's face.

With the players' good words in his ears, Al headed for the hotel and a good night's sleep. The next morning he got up early, feeling great. Tanimoto was still sleeping. Al decided to take a walk around town.

The hotel was still as he walked through the halls. None of the other players were up yet. Only the man behind the desk was awake.

Al walked out the door and took a deep breath of the clear early morning air. He stepped into the street to cross to the other side. Suddenly, a small blue truck came speeding toward him. For a moment, Al was afraid the truck was trying to run him over. He jumped out of the way as it screamed to a stop just beside him.

A young woman put her head out the truck window.

"Sanchez! I saw you in the game last night," the woman said. "You were really great!"

"Thanks," said Al. He waited by the truck, wondering if it would go flying off again.

The woman was shaking her head. "The way you scored! That poor catcher didn't know what was happening."

Al laughed. "Well, I guess he didn't see me coming."

"You can say that again," the woman went on. "Say, I'm Lucy Harper. I hope you're going to pull a few more moves in the second game against Coaxwood tonight."

"I hope to," Al said. "You going to be there?"

"Oh, sure," Lucy said. "I go to every home game. I'll be there tonight." She smiled and then hit the gas. The truck went racing on down the street.

"See you there," Al called after her. But his words were lost in the noise of the truck's engine.

The day moved slowly for Al. He saw the town swimming pool, the school, the few stores, and the town hall. He walked around, looking at everything. Then he ate in the diner. He waited for the night to come.

It started with a bang. As soon as he got to the locker room, he looked at the names on the starting lineup. He saw *Sanchez, A. Third base.* Waller was going to have him start.

"Willis is going to love sitting on the bench," Lou Clayton called as he saw Al checking the list.

"Oh, probably not," Al laughed back.

As the game was about to begin, Al took his place at third. Suddenly a woman wearing a Woodside Hawks baseball hat caught his eye. It was Lucy Harper. She was waving at him from the stands.

Al touched the front of his hat in answer. Then he looked toward the dugout. Scott Willis was sitting there with his arms folded. He was looking right at Al. It was plain that he wasn't at all happy to see Al standing in his spot at third. He's probably hoping I break a leg, Al thought.

Then the game started. The first Coaxwood batter singled to right. The second tapped a fine bunt down the line toward third base. Al raced for it, knowing he would have to hurry. He picked up the ball and fired it to first. The throw was low, pulling the first baseman off the bag. The Coaxwood runner had a single.

Al kicked the dirt. Only minutes into the game and Coaxwood had runners on first and second. Then things got worse. The third batter hit one that tore over Al's head into left field. A run scored. There was no way Al could have caught the ball. But he felt that he should have.

Then the pitcher settled down. The next batter struck out. The batter after him grounded into a double play. The score was 1–0 as the Hawks came to bat in the bottom of the first. As Al waited in the dugout, Lou Clayton handed him a piece of paper.

Al opened it. It said, *Hit me a home run tonight and I'll take you to a really great place. Lucy.*

Al laughed. He turned to Clayton. "Where did you get this?"

"One of your fans just handed it to me," Lou said. Then he added in a low voice, "Watch yourself. I think she might be something special to Scott Willis. I've seen her with him."

Just then, Al heard his name called. He went to the on-deck circle and waited there until it was his turn to bat. Then, with a quick step, he walked to the plate. He couldn't wait to knock the first ball that came his way out of the ball park.

CHAPTER 5

Stealing Home

The pitch came straight toward the plate, then sailed away high and outside. But Al had swung. He missed by a mile. He missed the next pitch too.

He had two strikes on him. Wait for the right pitch, he told himself with an angry shake of the head. He held back from swinging as the next ball flew toward him. It went in a straight line right into the catcher's glove.

"Strike," the umpire shouted. Al struck out on three pitches.

He struck out again on his next turn at bat. Then, later in the game, he came up with runners on first and second. He hit into a double play. By the bottom of the ninth, Al hadn't hit the ball past second base. Now, with the game tied 3–3, and with no one on and one out, Al was up again.

As he walked out of the dugout to pick up a bat, the fans were very still. Everyone was hoping for a win. But the Coaxwood pitcher was hot. And the Woodside bats were growing cold. Al knew he had to get a hit now. It could put the Hawks closer to a win. And it might keep Waller from putting him back on the bench for going without a hit.

He was headed for the plate when he heard Waller's voice.

"Sanchez!"

Al stopped short. Was Waller taking him out for a pinch hitter? The heavyset manager came slowly over to him. "Stop trying to put it out of the park every time you get up," Waller said to him. "You don't need a home run. Just get on base."

"OK," said Al. Suddenly he felt a lot better. And he began to feel like maybe this time he would get a hit. He turned and made his way to the plate.

The first pitch sailed away, high and outside. Al watched it go by.

"Ball," the umpire called.

Taking it slow pays off, Al remembered. You have to give yourself time to think.

Then Al had another idea. He looked around the field. The Coaxwood third baseman was playing him deep, back on the grass. He would have a long way to come in to reach a bunt. Al decided to lay one down the line.

The next pitch was good to bunt. It came in low, and Al tapped it down the line. It was a slow roller. There was no way the third baseman could get to it in time. Al raced across first as the angry third baseman came up with the ball.

Vern Biggs, the Hawks catcher, was up next. And the steal sign was on. Al didn't wait. On the first pitch, he broke hard for second. The throw from the Coaxwood catcher came in high as Al came in low. He was safe at second.

Suddenly Al felt better than he had all night. He loved to run, and he felt his heart pumping fast as he stepped off second base.

But the Coaxwood pitcher wasn't happy. He looked back at Al once, twice. Then he looked back at the plate and threw. The pitch was low and in the dirt. It almost got away from the catcher.

Al took a longer lead off second. He began to dance back and forth. People in the stands began to yell, "Go! Go! Go!" Then the Coaxwood pitcher threw again, and Al was running. He tore across the space between second and third and went into the bag head first. A small storm of dust went up around him. As the dust cleared away, the crowd could see that the third baseman's glove was right where it should have been—on Al's arm. But the ball wasn't in it. It had fallen out of his glove and lay on the ground a few inches away.

Al stood up and dusted himself off. The crowd went wild.

As Vern Biggs waited at home plate for the pitch, Al took a lead down the line. The third baseman moved in closer to the bag. Al knew the pitcher might try to pick him off at third. And that was what he was hoping for. If the pitcher made a move toward third, Al had a move of his own to make. He was going to break for home.

The sound of the crowd filled Al's ears. The Coaxwood pitcher eyed him and then turned toward home plate. Al took a few more steps down the line, knowing just how far he could go without getting picked off. Any second the throw could come. If it came, Al knew he wouldn't stop for anything.

Then it happened. The pitcher wheeled to throw to third. As soon as the ball left his hand, Al was off and running for the plate. Behind Al, the third baseman took the throw. He turned and fired toward home. Vern Biggs stayed in the batter's box as long as he could. The catcher had to jump to the side to field the throw. When Biggs stepped out of the box, the ball and Al were both reaching the plate at the same time. Al went into a slide. And the catcher jumped toward him for the tag.

Going Strong 6

Al slid hard, rolling to one side. He touched the bag as the catcher touched him. He could hear the crowd screaming as he wiped the dirt from his eyes. What would the call be?

Then the umpire waved his arms at his sides. Al was safe! The Woodside team came piling out of the dugout to pound him on the back. As they closed in, Al could hear the Coaxwood catcher shouting at the umpire, "But I had him! I had him!"

Someone else was as angry as the catcher. Gus Waller pushed his way into the circle of players around Al. His face was red. "Can't you do anything without a show? I told you to get on base, Sanchez," the manager said. "Not put on a circus act."

Waller stormed off again. But no one cared. The Hawks had won the game. And that was all that mattered.

After changing his clothes, Al left the crowded locker room. Lucy Harper was waiting outside. With a smile she said, "Well, that bunt wasn't a home run. But it did the trick. So I'll still take you out. How about Zeke's? It's the place to go. And I want to show you off."

"Zeke's it is," Al said as he walked with Lucy to her truck.

When they got to the small-town meeting place, the sound of loud music met them in the big parking lot. Lights burned in every window. Al could hear a lot of noise—loud voices and stamping feet. Lucy took his hand as they went in through the front door.

"Lucy!"

"Say, it's Al Sanchez!"

"Great game, Al!"

Everyone called out as Lucy and Al walked in. It looked as if everyone was having a great time. Al was laughing as he and Lucy joined some people in a corner of the room lined with

Hawks flags and pictures of racing cars. It was going to be a good night, Al thought. Everything was coming together for him.

In a few minutes, a few of the Woodside baseball players came in—Lou Clayton, Neal Tanimoto, and Vern Biggs. They all came over to kid around with Al. "You keep it up, and we'll be in first place," Biggs said to him. Lou said he thought so too. Neal Tanimoto gave Al a pat on the back. Soon the three players and the others at the table went out onto the floor to dance. Lucy and Al were left by themselves.

For several minutes they talked about themselves, about baseball, and about Lucy's plans to move one day to New York or Los Angeles. She wanted to get away from the little town of Woodside. As they talked, Scott Willis walked in the front door. He headed toward Lou Clayton and the other players. But when he reached the middle of the floor, he saw Al and Lucy. He stormed over.

"You're doing all right, Sanchez," he said in a slow, heavy voice. "First you take my job. Now you're working on Lucy."

Lucy looked from Willis to Al. She smiled. "Go to bed, Willis," said Al. "I think you've had too much to drink."

Willis tried to stand still as he stared at Al. The next thing Al knew, Willis was shouting, "Get on your feet!"

Al had had enough. He jumped up. Willis hit out at him. But Al ducked out of the way. Then he grabbed Willis by the arms and started to push him toward the door. When Clayton and Tanimoto saw what was happening, they came over and took hold of Willis.

"Come on, Willis," said Clayton, "Let's go home. This isn't your night." Clayton and Tanimoto steered an angry Willis out the front door.

Later, after a lot of talk and dancing, Lucy drove Al back to the hotel. On the way, he asked her about Willis. "Have you two really got something going? Have you gone out with him a lot?"

Lucy just laughed, and said, "Are you kidding? I went out with him a few times—when he first got to town. That was enough. I can do a lot better than that. And I am now." She stopped the truck outside the Prince Hotel. "I want to see you again," she said to Al. "I want to see a lot of you."

"You will," he said.

The next morning, Al saw Willis on the street. Willis walked past him without a word. That night, Al started at third again and Willis stayed on the bench. Waller might not have liked Al's way of making runs, but he knew Al could make them. And Al didn't let him down. He hit a home run and a double that drove in 3 runs. The Hawks won their third straight game, 6–3.

Over the next few weeks, Al got a lot more hits and stole more bases too. He made some poor plays at third, but his hitting more than made up for them. Waller kept him in the lineup. Willis stayed on the bench, filling in once in a while at third or shortstop. He never spoke to Al. But lots of other people did.

Al was becoming well known around Woodside. People smiled and said hello to him on the street. They came up to talk to him after the games. In Woodside, Al was somebody. That was something new for him. He hadn't felt that way since the time the big teams had been after him. Back in St. Louis, Al had just been a kid who had been in trouble. He had been someone no one wanted to know.

Now life moved on in a fast, happy way for Al. He saw a lot of Lucy Harper. They had fun seeing the sights and dancing at Zeke's. And as June turned into July, the Hawks moved into first place. Al kept out of trouble and saved a little money. He bought an old car and a few new clothes. It seemed that nothing could go wrong again.

Then one day, after the team had returned from a road trip, he got a call at the hotel. It was from Jane Henshaw, who wrote about sports for the *Woodside Tribune*. Henshaw wanted to write a story about Al.

"Great," Al said into the telephone. "I've always wanted to have someone write about me—you know, what I like to eat, where I grew up, all that silly stuff," he joked.

"That's not the story I had in mind," Henshaw told him. "Why don't you meet me tonight after the game, and we'll talk about it?"

CHAPTER 7

The Story Gets Out

"I hear you did some time in jail," Henshaw said to Al that night as Al stepped into her car after the game. The Hawks had won again. But now Al's heart jumped a beat. He had hoped that the story of his trouble in St. Louis would never make it to Woodside. How had Henshaw found out?

"It's true," Al said to Henshaw after a moment. "Who told you?"

"Word gets around," said Henshaw. "You want to talk about it?"

Al told the woman from the *Woodside Tribune* the whole story—his side as well as the police's. When he finished, Henshaw said, "It sounds as if you got a bad deal."

Al let out a deep breath. "I'm glad you see it that way," he said. "But I'd rather you didn't

39

write about it. I'm doing OK here. I'm making a fresh start and—"

"I'm sorry," said Henshaw, cutting him off. "My paper wants the story. You're a big name here. And my piece will interest a lot of people. I don't want to hurt you, Al. I'll make the story fair. But I have to do my job."

The next day, the *Tribune* came out with the story. *Al Sanchez Tries Again* ran across the top of the front page.

The lines that followed said, "Al Sanchez, the hard-hitting Hawks third baseman, is making a fresh start here in Woodside. So far, it's working out. But only a year ago, Sanchez was in deep trouble. The St. Louis police arrested him on charges of. . . ."

The story went on to tell about Al's arrest and the time he served in jail. It gave both sides of the story. But the word on Al's bad time was out. As Al sat reading the paper in his hotel room, a call came in for him from Gus Waller.

"See me in my office" was all the manager said.

A few minutes later, Al and Waller were face to face. Al had never seen Waller so mad.

"Are you crazy? Talking to Henshaw like that," Waller shouted at him. "This is going to make a lot of trouble for you—and for the team. Why in the world did you tell her?"

"I didn't tell her. She already knew," said Al.

Waller stared hard at Al. "Then *who* told her? I didn't. And I thought I was the only one who knew."

Al left Waller's office and went back to the hotel. As he walked, he had a strange feeling. He thought that people were looking at him in a different way. "You're crazy," he said to himself. But that night he found out that he wasn't.

The Tarboro White Sox were in town for an important game with the Hawks. Tarboro had been in first place until the Hawks had knocked them out of it. Now they were in second place, only two games behind Woodside. They wanted to get even.

As the game started, the Tarboro players on the bench did a lot of yelling at the Hawks on the field. Al made a bad play on the first ball that was hit to him. It was an easy grounder. But it went through his legs and into left field.

As Al ran after the ball, a Tarboro player called, "Hey, Sanchez! What are you high on tonight?" Then another one shouted, "Know where I can get a good deal on some drugs?" A lot of players laughed—even some guys on Al's team.

When Al came to bat, a lot of boos were heard from the Woodside people in the stands. Al looked up at them and shook his head. He couldn't believe that they would turn against him so quickly.

To make things worse, he struck out on only three pitches. Someone in the stands yelled, "Hey, Sanchez, why don't you go back to jail?" Everyone near the man laughed.

The next time Al was up, he struck out again. Later he made another bad play at third. He was too keyed up to play well. And the crowd kept after him. On his third time up, he popped up to the catcher. The same man in the stands who had called out before shouted, "Where did you learn to hit like that, Sanchez? In jail?"

Finally it was the bottom of the ninth. The Hawks were up. They were behind 5–3. A runner was on first and there were two outs as

Al walked up to bat. A home run would tie the game, and Al was swinging to put one over the fence. He wanted to show everyone how well he could hit. And he did. He ripped the first pitch down the line toward the fence. But it curved foul at the last second.

The next pitch came in high and inside— and sailed toward Al's head. Al hit the dirt. When he got up, he was mad. He started to go out after the man, but he held back. He knew he didn't need any more trouble. Instead, he gave the pitcher a look that said, "Try that again and I'll knock your head off."

But the fans had to rub it in. The same man in the stands called, "Sanchez is mad! Lock him up!" Again, some of the people around him laughed.

The next pitch came in. Al held back, but the umpire called it a strike. The count had gone to one and two. And the Tarboro pitcher was winding up. The bat didn't feel right in Al's hands. But the pitch was on its way.

As the ball sailed toward the plate, it looked good to Al. Too good. He swung—and hit the empty air. It was over. Al was out, and Tarboro had won the game, 5–3.

As Al threw his bat to the ground, he heard the voice in the stands again. The man shouted, "Now you can go back to jail, Sanchez! Three strikes, you're out!"

Something inside Al gave way. He had had enough. He threw off his hat and ran to the low fence that circled the field. He jumped over it onto the first row of seats. He kept on going to the middle of the stands, looking for the man who had done all the shouting.

But he couldn't find him. No one in the stands was shouting now. Everyone was still, staring at him. Al couldn't take it. He

shouted, "What was so funny? Nothing's funny now, is it? What's wrong with you people?"

Suddenly he felt a pair of hands grab him from behind. He turned and tried to break free. Lou Clayton was holding him. Lou shouted, "Come on, Al! Take it easy!"

Then Neal Tanimoto came up and helped Lou hold on to Al. In a second, Al stopped fighting, and Neal and Lou walked with him down to the field. No one said a word as the three players walked toward the locker room.

"Nice going, Sanchez," Gus Waller said as Al fell onto a bench. "I'm going to have to fine you $100 for that act."

Al said nothing. He dressed quickly and spoke to no one. Just as he was leaving, Lou Clayton came up to him. "Not everyone feels like those crazy people," Lou said. "Do you want to talk?"

"No," said Al. "Thanks. But I want to be alone."

He headed for his car. Lucy Harper stood next to it.

"Don't worry about those people, Al," she said. "Jail is no big deal. Just forget about it."

But Al couldn't forget about it. He told Lucy that he would rather be by himself that night. Lucy shook her head and moved off toward her truck and Zeke's.

Al started driving, trying to work through his hurt. He wanted to get off the team and get out of Woodside. His hands shook as they held the wheel. Without knowing it, he started going faster and faster. Soon he saw a police car coming up behind him. Its red light was turning, telling Al to pull over.

Al drove to the side of the road. The police car pulled over too. In a moment, two police officers were at his window.

"Well, if it isn't Al Sanchez. You're driving too fast," said one officer. Then the other officer asked Al to step out of the car. "We have a search warrant," he said. "We have to look inside your car."

Al stared out at them. "What for?"

"We'll worry about that," said the first officer. "Step outside." Then he said to the other man, "Take a good look inside, George."

One More Time 8

Al stood on the road as one officer looked at him and the other looked through his car. He couldn't believe it was happening.

Minutes went by. Then suddenly the man in the car said, "I think I've found something." He came out of the car holding a small bag. "Looks like speed."

The first officer shook his head as he looked at Al. "Going back into the drug business, Sanchez?"

Al wanted to run—or scream. But there was nothing he could do. He just couldn't make himself believe it had happened. Who would want to put that stuff in his car?

Then Al felt himself being moved toward the police car. "Better come with us, Sanchez," one officer was saying. "We need to talk about this." In seconds, Al was on his way to the Woodside police station.

"Well, the tip was right," the officer behind the wheel said. "We got a call tonight about you. Someone said if we looked in your car, we would find drugs."

Al sat up. "Who called you?"

"The person didn't give a name," the officer said. "But what difference does it make? The tip was right, wasn't it?"

The police station was dark and gray. After Al was booked, he was told he could make one telephone call. He thought about calling Lucy Harper. But then he decided to call Frank Martino in St. Louis instead.

"The stuff wasn't mine," he told Martino over the telephone. "I never saw it before. Someone down here is out to get me."

"All right," said Martino. "Take it easy. I'll be down in the morning to get you out."

After Martino had hung up, Al just stood there with the telephone in his hand. He wondered if even Frank Martino would believe him this time.

The night moved slowly, and Al didn't get much sleep. He kept seeing it happen all over again. The red light of the police car. The two officers. The bag. *Someone said if we looked in your car. . . .*

Soon after the sun came up, Frank Martino came to the jail. Once he had paid Al's bail, Al was free to go. Outside the jail Jane Henshaw, the woman from the *Woodside Tribune,* was waiting for him.

"I heard what happened," Henshaw said. "I hope my story didn't have anything to do with it."

Al shook his head. "Who knows?" he said.

Al told Henshaw everything about the night before. Then he and Frank Martino headed for the diner to have breakfast.

"I spoke with Gus Waller this morning," Martino told Al. "I called him before I left home. He likes the way you've been playing ball. But I'm afraid you're off the team. And there's no way you can get back with them. I just hope you don't have to go back to jail."

Al looked into his cup. He didn't know what to do or what to say. He and Frank Martino sat without talking.

Finally Martino spoke. "Why don't you come back to St. Louis for a while? I could—"

Al sat up and cut him off. "No," he said. "I'm not going back to St. Louis. I'm not going to jail either. I'm going to stay here and find out who set me up. I like it here too much to let myself be run off."

Martino moved forward in his chair. "OK," he said. "I'm with you. Any idea who could have done it?"

"My first thought is that Scott Willis did it—the guy whose job I took away," Al said.

Martino nodded slowly. "Then start with him. But watch yourself, Al. You don't need any more trouble. And let me know if I can help."

Martino paid the bill, and the two men went to the Prince Hotel. Al's old manager had some calls to make, and Al needed time to think. Al wasn't in his room long before someone knocked at the door. It was Lou Clayton.

"I saw you come in, Al," he said. "I want to talk with you."

"You're about the only one who still will," Al said with a small laugh. "What's up?"

"I think maybe Scott Willis set you up."

Al closed the door behind Lou and walked to the middle of the room.

"It's just an idea," Lou went on. "But I was in Zeke's one night last week, and Willis was there. He was a little out of his head. But it wasn't from anything he had been drinking. I could tell. He was on something like speed. He kept talking. He kept saying over and over again that he was going to 'fix' you."

Al beat his fingers on the back of the chair. "Did he say how?"

"No," said Lou. "He talked a lot. But most of it was pretty wild. All but what he said about you. He kept saying that he would 'fix' you and that you would 'get the picture.'" Lou Clayton shook his head. "There isn't much more to tell you. I just thought you should know."

"Well, thanks for coming by," Al told Lou. "You're a good friend."

Lou headed for the door. "What are you going to do now, Al?"

After a moment, Al said, "I'm going back to St. Louis tonight."

The two players shook hands, and Lou walked down the hall.

Al finished cleaning out his room. Then he called Jane Henshaw at the *Tribune*. "I want to see you tonight," Al said. "I've got another story for you. Could you meet me at nine?"

"The Hawks have a game tonight," Henshaw answered. "I need to cover it. I'll meet you after it's over, say around 10 o'clock."

"No. I have to see you before it's over," Al told her.

"Why?"

"I'll explain later," said Al. "But it's important. Can you get away early and meet me at nine?"

"All right," said Henshaw. "Where?"

"I'll meet you on the other side of town in the parking lot of the T-Bone Diner. Don't be late. And don't tell anyone you're meeting me," Al said.

"I'll be there," Henshaw told him before she hung up.

Since Al was out on bail, he had to let the police know he was leaving town. He called the station and told them he was going back to St. Louis for a few days. Then he called Lucy Harper to tell her the same thing. She didn't answer her telephone, and Al thought that she was probably out with someone new. He hadn't called her since last night, when he had told her he wanted to be by himself. And she wasn't one to wait around.

Later that afternoon, Al followed Frank Martino out of town on the road to St. Louis. But when they got about 20 miles outside of town, Al hit the horn and headed back to Woodside. On the way, he stopped for dinner. Then, at nine o'clock, he pulled into the parking lot at the T-Bone Diner, turned off the engine, and waited for Henshaw.

Clearing the Fence 9

Al waited in the parking lot. Soon it was 9:15, and there was no sign of Henshaw. He began to worry. Where was she?

Suddenly Al had more to worry about. A police car turned into the parking lot and pulled up beside him. Out stepped two police officers—the same two who had arrested him the night before.

The one named George put his head through Al's open window. "What are you doing around here, Sanchez? We thought you were headed back to St. Louis."

"I am," Al said. "I just stopped here to get some dinner."

The police officers looked at Al for a long time. He could see they weren't sure they should believe his story.

"All right," George said finally. "But watch yourself. Woodside is a fine little town. We don't want you making any more trouble around here."

The two men walked slowly back to their car, got in, and drove off. As they left, Al got out of his car and made it look as if he were going inside to eat. When the police were out of sight, he got back into his car. His watch showed 9:25.

Suddenly, a crazy thought crossed his mind. *Henshaw* must have told the police where to find him. She must have decided that Al was up to something. Al just shook his head. Then he saw Henshaw's car pull into the lot. He got out and walked quickly over to her car.

"Sorry I'm late," Henshaw said. "It was hard to get away. What's this all about?"

"You'll see." Al climbed into the car beside Henshaw. "We're going to take a little trip into town. I want to check something out at the hotel."

Henshaw looked surprised, but she drove toward town. As she did, Al kept looking back. He was afraid they were being followed by the police.

"OK," Henshaw said after a minute. "Now you need to tell me a little more about what's happening."

"Someone set me up last night," said Al. "I think it was Scott Willis."

"If you were set up, Willis would be one person who would want to do it," said Henshaw. "He was the one who told me about your jail record. But can you prove Willis set you up?"

"I don't know," said Al. "But I have an idea that I'll find some drugs in his hotel room. That's where we're headed now—to check it out before the game is over and he comes back. If I find some, I may be able to force him into telling how he set me up."

Henshaw took a quick look at Al. "Why do you want me along? Shouldn't you have called the police?"

"They would never believe me," Al said. "And they sure wouldn't let me into Willis's room. If you're with me and I find something, the police will believe you."

Henshaw nodded. "And I'll have a story for tomorrow's paper."

They drove on for a minute without speaking. Then Henshaw added, "Of course, you know you'll be breaking the law."

Al nodded. "I know. It's kind of funny—breaking the law to prove you didn't break the law."

When they got to town, Henshaw drove the car to the back of the hotel. Al got out and headed for the fire escape. As Henshaw walked around to the front door, Al climbed up to the third floor. Pushing up the window of Willis's room, he climbed inside.

After a few minutes, a knock sounded at the door. Al went to it and let Henshaw in. With Al's flashlight, the two of them began looking through the room.

But 20 minutes later, they had found nothing. "We should get out of here," Henshaw said. "The game should be over by now. Willis will be coming back soon."

"Wait," said Al. "Just a few more minutes. Please."

"I can't," said Henshaw. "I can't take the chance of being caught in here." And she was out the door and gone.

Again Al hunted through the room. Again he found nothing. He was about to give up when the circle of light from his flashlight fell onto the wall just above Willis's bed. There, in the circle of light, was a picture of a train crossing a wide river. Al remembered Lou Clayton's words. *He kept saying that he would 'fix' you and that you would 'get the picture.'*

The picture! That had to be it! Al tore the picture from the wall. He had just forced open the back of the picture and found the small bags inside when the door opened. Scott Willis walked in and turned on the light.

Willis stared at him. "What are you doing here?"

"You set me up," said Al. "You planted the speed in my car."

"I don't know what you're talking about," said Willis. "You're crazy."

Al pointed to the picture where it lay on the bed. "What about the picture then? What about what's inside it?"

Suddenly Willis swung at Al. He knocked him against the wall. Al held his side and tried to get up. He couldn't.

Willis stood over him with a lamp in one hand. "You know, you were right, Sanchez. I set you up. I wanted to get back at you for taking my job and making me sit on the bench. And for taking out Lucy." Willis shook his head."But no one is ever going to know. I'll get rid of the drugs. And I'll get the police myself. No one will think twice about it if I tell them I knocked out someone who broke into my room."

As he lifted his arm, the door opened. Henshaw and Lou Clayton ran into the room. "Forget it, Willis," said Clayton.

"He broke in here," said Willis. "I was just going to—"

"You're not going to do anything," Henshaw told him. "We heard the whole story through the door."

The next day, the charges against Al were dropped. Instead, Scott Willis was placed under arrest.

Two nights later, Al was back on the field for the Hawks. But Lucy Harper wasn't in the stands. Some of her friends told Al that she had left town. Al might have missed her. But he was playing the best game he had played in a long time.

The score was tied late in the game as Al came up to bat. After taking the sign from the catcher, the pitcher took one last look at Al and threw. It was a high, hard fastball—Al's kind of pitch. He swung hard. The bat made a loud crack, and Al watched the ball as it headed out to deep left. It cleared the fence and kept on going.

The people in the stands were on their feet. They were cheering Al once again. Even Gus Waller was smiling. As he crossed third, Al saw the heavyset manager on the dugout steps. With a smile of his own, Al made the turn and headed for home.